Hurricanes

Ted O'Hare

Bethany, Missouri

Photo Credits:
Cover © P.I.R.; Title page © Daniel Gustavsson; Page 4 © Lorenzo Puricelli; Pages 6, 22 © Peter Blottman;
Page 7 © Steve Shoup; Page 8 © Ingrid E Stamatson, Robert A. Mansker, G. Lewis; Page 9 © G Lewis, Tad Denson;
Pages 12, 13 © Lisa F. Young; Page 14 © Patsy Lynch/FEMA; Page 15 © Marvin Nauman/FEMA photo; Page 16 ©
NWS; Page 19 © Winn Henderson / FEMA; Page 20 © FEMA News Photo; Page 21 © FEMA News Photo,
Marvin Nauman/FEMA photo

Cataloging-in-Publication Data

O'Hare, Ted, 1961-
     Hurricanes / Ted O'Hare. — 1st ed.
     p. cm. — (Natural disasters)

     Includes bibliographical references and index.
     Summary: Illustrations and text introduce hurricanes,
from their history and causes, to how they are measured
and where they occur.
     ISBN-13: 978-1-4242-1401-3 (lib. bdg. : alk. paper)
     ISBN-10: 1-4242-1401-7 (lib. bdg. : alk. paper)
     ISBN-13: 978-1-4242-1491-4 (pbk. : alk. paper)
     ISBN-10: 1-4242-1491-2 (pbk. : alk. paper)

     1. Hurricanes—Juvenile literature. [1. Hurricanes.
2. Natural disasters.] I. O'Hare, Ted, 1961- II. Title.
III. Series.
     QC944.2.O43 2007
     551.55'2—dc22

First edition
© 2007 Fitzgerald Books
802 N. 41st Street, P.O. Box 505
Bethany, MO 64424, U.S.A.
Printed in China
Library of Congress Control Number: 2006940885

Table of Contents

What Makes a Hurricane?

A hurricane begins as a small **tropical** thunderstorm. It then becomes a tropical **depression**, which grows into a large and very windy storm.

Warm ocean water is needed to make a tropical depression. This warm water causes the air to rise. Cool air moves in and replaces the warm air.

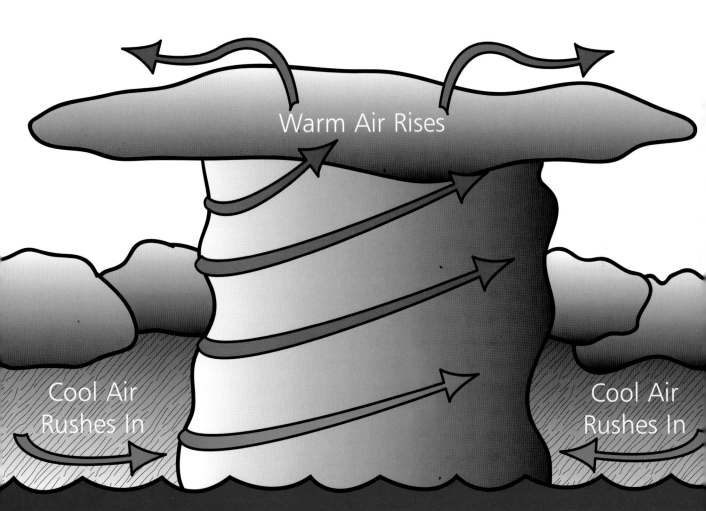

Warm Air Rises

Cool Air
Rushes In

Cool Air
Rushes In

Warm Ocean Water (80°)

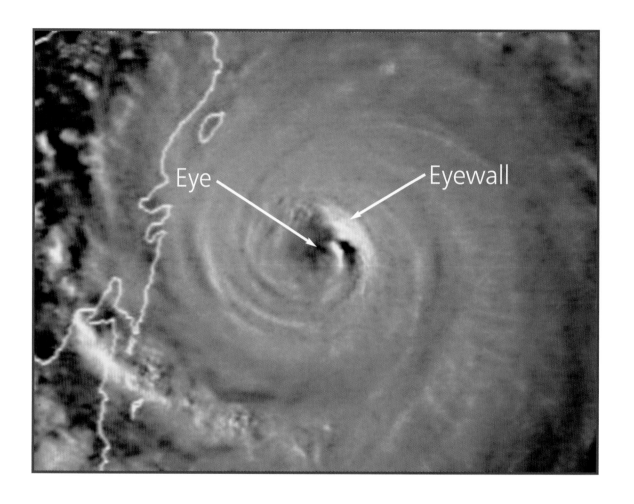

The eye of a hurricane is at the center. Then comes the **eyewall**. This is a column of clouds that surrounds the eye. Beyond the eyewall is a group of rainbands.

Strong winds and heavy rainfall usually accompany a hurricane. Flooding may also occur. Funnels of blowing wind often follow, sometimes causing tornadoes.

When the storm force increases, hurricanes can cause much damage. Houses and businesses can be destroyed. And there may be injuries and even

Hurricane Season

Most hurricanes occur from June 1 through November 30. Areas most affected are the Atlantic Ocean, the Gulf of Mexico, and the Caribbean Sea.

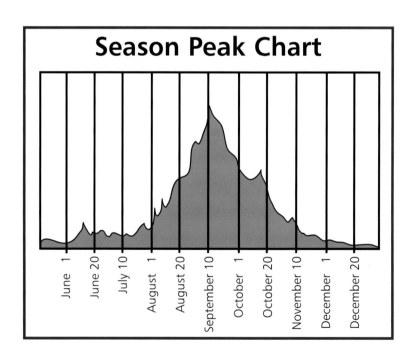

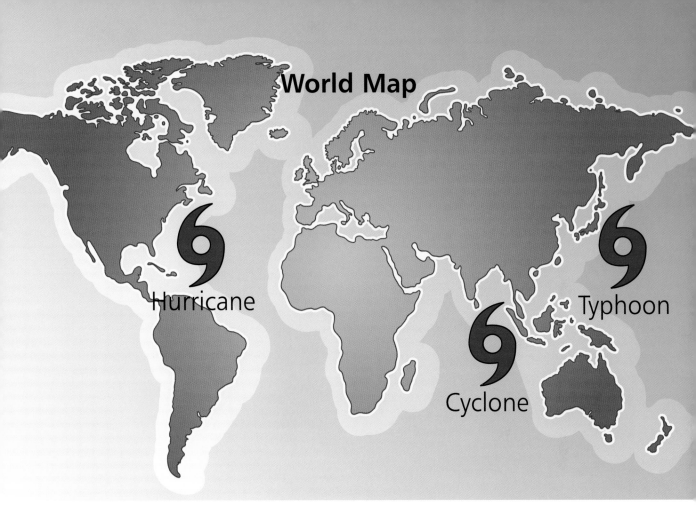

World Map

Hurricane

Cyclone

Typhoon

In some parts of the world these storms are known as **cyclones** or **typhoons**. Typhoons occur in the Pacific Ocean. Cyclones are storms that occur in the Indian Ocean.

Hurricane Preparedness

Before a hurricane comes, it is a good idea to prepare for the storm. It is good to have extra supplies of food, water, and gas. The best plan is to leave before the hurricane comes.

Measuring a Hurricane

To become a hurricane, a storm must reach **sustained** winds of 74 miles per hour (119 km).

Meteorologists give hurricanes ratings to tell people how strong the storm is.

The Saffir-Simpson Scale tells the wind speed of a hurricane.

Saffir-Simpson Scale		
Category One:	74 - 95 mph	(119-153 km/hr)
Category Two:	96 - 110 mph	(154-177 km/hr)
Category Three:	111 - 130 mph	(178-209 km/hr)
Category Four:	131 - 155 mph	(210-249 km/hr)
Category Five:	156 mph or greater	(250 km/hr or greater)

Naming a Hurricane

The U. S. National Weather Service names hurricanes for easy identification. Both women's and men's names are used in a six-year cycle. The letters Q, U, X, Y, and Z are not used.

Atlantic Hurricane Names

Andrea	Arthur
Barry	Bertha
Chantal	Cristobal
Dean	Dolly
Erin	Edouard
Felix	Fay
Gabrielle	Gustav
Humberto	Hanna
Ingrid	Ike
Jerry	Josephine
Karen	Kyle
Lorenzo	Lili
Melissa	Marco
Noel	Nana
Olga	Omar
Pablo	Paloma
Rebekah	Rene
Sebastien	Sally
Tanya	Teddy
Van	Vicky
Wendy	Wilfred

Famous Hurricanes

Hurricane Katrina is the most destructive hurricane in recent history. It hit the Gulf Coast of the United States in August 2005. Katrina destroyed much of the coastal regions of Louisiana, Mississippi, and Alabama.

About 1,300 people lost their lives as a result of Katrina.

19

One of the most horrible early hurricanes killed 8,000 to 12,000 people in and around Galveston, Texas, in 1900. And many people still remember the damage caused in Florida by Hurricane Andrew in 1992.

New Hurricanes

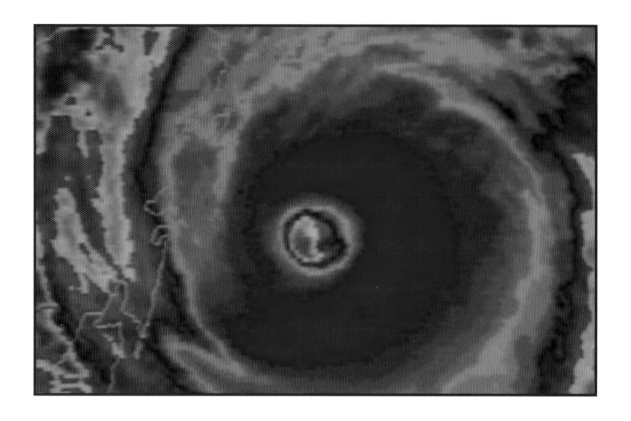

Meteorologists now have a great deal of new technology: radar, computer models, and satellites. These help people watch and better predict where and when hurricanes will strike.

Glossary

cyclones (SY klonz) — hurricanes that occur in the Indian Ocean

depression (dee PRESH un) — an area of low pressure made up of mostly warm air

eyewall (EYE wawl) — a column of clouds surrounding a hurricane's eye

meteorologists (MEE tee uh rol uh jistz) — people who study weather and climate

sustained (sus TAYND) — maintained for a period of time without weakening

tropical (TROP uh kul) — occurring within the two Tropic lines on the globe

typhoons (tie FOONZ) — hurricanes that occur in the northern Pacific Ocean

Index

FURTHER READING

Demarest, Chris L. *Hurricane Hunters: Riders on the Storm*. Margaret K. McElderry
  Books, 2006.
Langley, Andrew. *Hurricanes, Tsunamis and Other Natural Disasters*. Kingfisher, 2006.
Simon, Seymour. *Hurricanes*. HarperCollins, 2003.

WEBSITES TO VISIT

Because Internet links change so often, Fitzgerald Books has developed an online list of websites related to the subject of this book. This site is updated regularly. Please use this link to access the list: www.fitzgeraldbookslinks.com/nd/hur

ABOUT THE AUTHOR

Ted O'Hare is an author and editor of children's nonfiction books. Ted has written over fifty children's books over the past decade. Ted has worked for many publishing houses including the Macmillan Children's Book Group.